RACHEL ISADORA

The Pirates of Bedford Street

Greenwillow Books

New York

Watercolors were used for the full-color art.
The text type is Korinna.

Copyright © 1988 by Rachel Isadora Turner
All rights reserved. No part of this book
may be reproduced or utilized in any form
or by any means, electronic or mechanical,
including photocopying, recording or by
any information storage and retrieval
system, without permission in writing
from the Publisher, Greenwillow Books,
a division of William Morrow & Company, Inc.,
105 Madison Avenue, New York, N.Y. 10016.
Printed in Hong Kong by South China Printing Co.
First Edition   10 9 8 7 6 5 4 3 2 1

Library of Congress Cataloging in Publication Data

Isadora, Rachel.
The pirates of Bedford Street.
Summary: After Joey and his sisters see a pirate
movie at the movie theater, the adventures of Captain
Redbeard continue—if only in Joey's imagination.
1. Children's stories, American.
[1. Pirates—Fiction.   2. Motion pictures—Fiction.
3. Imagination—Fiction.]   I. Title.
PZ7.I763Pi 1988   [E]   84-25904
ISBN 0-688-05206-1
ISBN 0-688-05208-8 (lib. bdg.)

FOR MY MOTHER RITA,

MY UNCLE JOE,

AND MY AUNT LEE

It's summer, and it's Saturday afternoon. There is a long
line in front of the Bedford Street movie theater.

Joey is almost always the first one there.

He hurries to his favorite seat in the tenth row.

He saves two seats for his sisters Rita and Lee.
The theater lights dim. Joey sits up tall.

"Watch out, Redbeard!" Joey shouts. "They're after you!"
"Shhhh!" someone says.

"Sit down," Rita whispers, and pulls him into his seat.

When the movie is over, everyone rushes out into the bright sunlight. Joey stops in front of a poster of Redbeard.

"Come on, Joey," Rita calls. "Mama told you to come straight home."

Joey kneels down and starts drawing
on the sidewalk with his chalk.
". . . and they sailed for many days,"
he says to himself.
"Joey, Papa will be home soon,"
Rita calls from the corner.

Joey finally joins his sisters, but
in his mind the story goes on —
"... *at last the pirates sight land.*
Redbeard lowers a boat and rows toward shore."

When they get home, Joey says, "I'll wait
out here for Papa."
He starts to draw again.
" . . . The pirates spot Redbeard.
'Get him! Get him before he gets the treasure!'
shouts Captain Blackhawk."

"Look at Joey. He's talking to himself!"
 Ralph says.
"He's talking to the sidewalk," Charlie says,
 and laughs.
"Want to go to the park with us?" Ralph asks.
"No, I'm waiting for my papa," Joey says.

"See you tomorrow, Joey," say Ralph and Charlie.

"Joey, look what you've done!" Mrs. Miller, the landlady, is standing over him.
"Every week when you come from the movies it's the same thing. I've told you time and time again not to draw on the building or the sidewalk. This time I'm going to tell your father. Get the bucket and scrubbing brush from the basement and wash it all off."

"Joey, are you getting the bucket?"

"Yes, Mrs. Miller," Joey calls from the basement.

*" . . . Captain Blackhawk and his men
row after Redbeard."*

" . . . Redbeard reaches the cave!"

"Joey!"
"Papa!"

Joey and Papa have a long talk.
Then Papa helps him clean up —
first the basement and then
the sidewalk and steps.

Mrs. Miller comes outside.
"Well done," she says. She gives Joey
a box of crayons and a drawing pad.
"Now when you draw you can keep
your pictures," she says.

It's Saturday again and the movie is over.
"Hurry, Joey," Rita and Lee are shouting.
"Coming," Joey calls. "Coming."